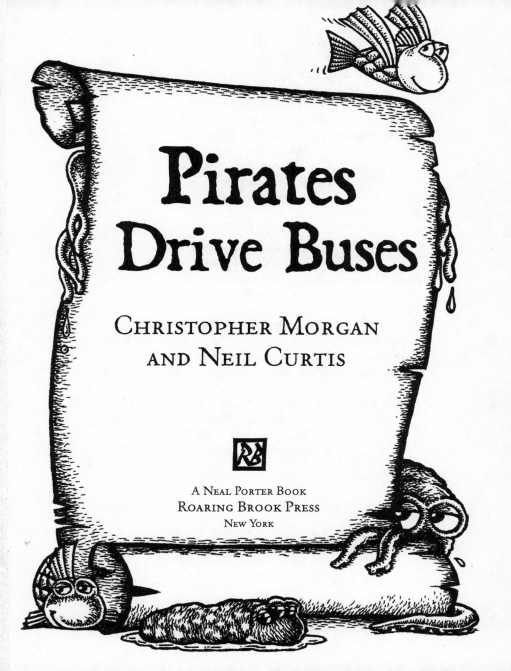

Pirates
Drive Buses

Christopher Morgan
and Neil Curtis

A Neal Porter Book
Roaring Brook Press
New York

Distributed in Canada by H. B. Fenn and Company, Ltd.

Library of Congress Cataloging-in-Publication Data
Morgan, Christopher, 1956-
Pirates drive buses / Christopher Morgan and [illustrated by] Neil Curtis.
— 1st American ed.
p. cm.
"A Neal Porter book."
Summary: While conducting a tour of the "landlubbers' world" for a bus
load of sea creatures, Pirate intercepts school-bound siblings Billy and
Heidi and enlists their aid in recovering his hijacked ship from
a troupe of mischievous monkey-crabs.
ISBN-13: 978-1-59643-313-7   ISBN-10: 1-59643-313-2
[1. Pirates—Fiction. 2. Marine animals—Fiction. 3. Humorous stories.]
I. Curtis, Neil, 1950- ill.   II. Title.
PZ7.M821137Pi 2008   [E]—dc22   2007002170

Roaring Brook Press books are available for special promotions
and premiums.
For details, contact: Director of Special Markets, Holtzbrinck Publishers.

Printed in the United States of America
First American edition March 2008
2 4 6 8 10 9 7 5 3 1

This story is for Victoria, Neil,
Claudia, and Chris.
—CM

Billy and Heidi were walking to school. They were in the middle of the World Championship Pinecone Kicking Contest when they heard the strangest sound.

A great yellow bus screeched to a halt beside them.

"Oh no," said Heidi. "It's that pirate again."

And she was right.

The door to the bus clattered open, and out leaped the pirate.

"What are *you* doing here?" asked Heidi.

"Great claws of crab! Didn't you get my letter? I told you I was coming."

"A letter?" said Billy. "When did you send it?"

"Ten minutes ago," said the pirate. "The mail must be slow today.

"Not to worry—you're here now. And so am I. Now **hurry up!**"

"Hurry up?" said Billy.

"Get on!" roared the pirate. "Get a move on! I'm running a tight ship, you know. And nobody likes **a squiddly slowpoke.**"

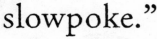

"We're on our way to school," said Heidi. "We're not coming with you." Heidi was good at school. Especially mathematics and spelling. And computers. And geography. And all the other subjects.

Billy was good at playtime.

"School!" said the pirate. "Blister me eyeballs, you can't go to school! We have a tour to run.

"Miss Fishnose, I'll write a note to the teacher and say you're not coming. We can mail it, and it will be there in five minutes."

He thumped the side of the bus.

"Now lift the seaweed anchor! Last one on is a sea-snail's hanky."

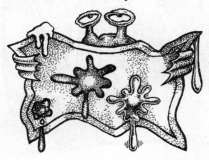

"I'm not sure about this," said Heidi.

"I am," said the pirate. "And one person being sure is all we need. Especially since I am a pirate and a bus driver."

"That doesn't make any sense," said Heidi.

"Miss Fishnose," said the pirate, "sense is for seagulls."

Heidi crossed her arms. "Well, I'm not coming."

But Billy was already halfway up the stairs. "I didn't really want to go to school today anyway," he said.

Heidi ground her teeth and followed Billy.

The pirate cheered. Just before they stepped through the doorway he whispered, "And be nice to the passengers."

Inside the bus, the seats were full of
all kinds of sea creatures. There were
octopuses and crabs, prawns and sea
horses. A South Sea walrus lay across the
backseat, and a large sea turtle crouched
in the aisle. Starfish pressed up against
the windows.

A small pig was perched on top of the driver's seat. When he saw Heidi, he leaped through the air and landed on her shoulder.

"Polly," said the pirate to the pig, "get that sea turtle back into his seat, like a good little parrot."

"Hello, Polly," said Heidi. "There's a good little pi . . ."

Billy nudged her. Heidi swallowed hard.

"A good little . . . parrot. It's nice to see you again."

"Twoink," said Polly, and nuzzled against Heidi's cheek. Then he scampered down the aisle and sat on the sea turtle's back.

There was another pirate halfway down the bus's aisle. He was serving a plate of seaweed to an octopus.

"That's my hostess, Frank Fellover," said the pirate. "He's doing a very good job today of not falling overboard."

The pirate cleared his throat, stamped his foot, and held his hand over his heart. **"Attention, passengers!"** he cried. "What we have here are two children. One is a girl." He poked Heidi. "And one is a boy." He did the same to Billy.

"Now please remember that they are very shy and very scared. They are not very smart, either. So try not to frighten them. And don't touch! Watch out for the girl in particular. She hasn't bitten anybody yet, but she may try."

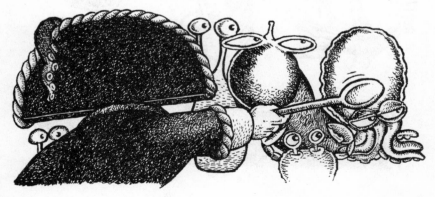

The sea creatures giggled.

"Now that's enough squiddling
about. It's time we continued the tour."

He sat down in the driver's seat and
revved the engine.

"And here . . . we . . . go!"

The bus lurched forward. The pirate didn't drive like Dad did. He spent most of his time tooting the horn with his toes and singing loudly.

"Where did you learn to drive a bus?" asked Billy. He could feel a lot of eyes on him. Heidi could feel them, too.

"Pirate Pirate Pirate School, of course," said the pirate. "I used to drive the Pirate School bus. I was very good at it. The secret to good bus driving is to keep your eyes closed as much as possible."

"Can you drive a bus, Mr. Fishcake?"

"No," said Billy. "I'm not old enough to drive a bus."

"What a lot of blabble bottom!" said the pirate. "Nobody is old enough to drive a bus. Nobody. Besides, all you need to know are the road rules. And I know them both. I'll teach them to you, and then you can drive."

"There are more than two rules," said Heidi. "Mom pays attention to all of them every time she drives."

"What sort of a bus does she drive?" asked the pirate.

"She doesn't drive a bus. She drives a car."

"Different set of rules for cars," said the pirate. "Only two for buses."

"Okay. What are they?" asked Billy. He wanted to drive a bus.

"Rule number one," said the pirate.
"You must not wash your clothes
while driving a bus."

He clicked his tongue loudly.

"Rule number two. You must never try to say your name into a bucket of water while you are driving a bus. **Never.**"

"I know both of the rules off by heart. I'm a champion."

"I'm a champion at kickball," said Heidi. "I won a medal."

"A medal!" said the pirate. "Is that all? I won a cabbage. I wore it around my neck for a year. Yes, I am a kickball champion, too. There's no question about it."

Heidi glared at him. "What team do you play for?" she asked. "And where do you play?"

"I play for the Pirate Hot Potatoes.
And we play on Big Toe Island."

"Who do you play against, then?"

"Nobody," said the pirate. "That way
we get the ball more often."

"That's not kickball," yelled Heidi.

"Oh yes it is, Miss Fishnose. I'm a bus
driver and a pirate. I know everything."
He wobbled his head proudly. "And I'm
a kickball champion."

"You're a pirate! Not a kickball champion. Or a bus driver! Why are you here? And where's your ship?"

Billy stepped between Heidi and the pirate. "Don't all pirates have a ship?" he asked politely.

"What sort of a landlubber question is that?" said the pirate. "Of course I have a ship, Mr. Fishcake. Now you tell that sister of yours to keep her voice down. There are parrots present, you know." He pointed to Polly.

Heidi squealed in fury.

"That—is—a—pig!" she said.

The pirate ignored her. "My ship is called the SS *You Beauty*. It's the fastest ship this side of that side." He saluted as he said the ship's name.

Frank Fellover saluted, too. Then he fell over sideways.

"We're looking for it, didn't you know? But the SS *You Beauty* has been stolen." The pirate frowned fiercely.

Billy frowned, too. But he couldn't help looking down the bus's aisle, away from the pirate. An octopus was bouncing up and down on a seat, and a popcorn starfish was hurtling happily from one side of the bus to the other.

Suddenly the pirate jammed his foot on the horn.

"Attention, passengers!" he bellowed. **"We are now passing a very interesting landmark."**

The sea creatures twittered, and everybody peered out the window.

"Over on our left," said the pirate, "we have what is called a soupymarket. It's where landlubbers go to buy their food.

"That's exactly right! They buy it! They don't even try to look under rocks or in old tins or in wormholes to get it themselves. Amazing!"

"But the excitement doesn't end there, passengers!" cried the pirate. "If you look up ahead, you can see a swimminy pool, where landlubbers learn to swim. It's the same sort of place as where you go to learn to walk."

An octopus started to walk up and down the aisle, its legs going everywhere. It climbed on top of seats, across the head of the blue-speckled mudskipper, and all over Frank Fellover, who had fallen over.

"Go back to your seat, Mr. Octopus," said the pirate. "Stop showing off."

Everybody was getting more and more excited. The octopuses were shaking hands with each other. The starfish were bouncing off the walls. The blue-speckled mudskipper was thumping his tail on the floor, and the pearl sea turtle was talking loudly to himself.

"Where are we going? They're all so excited." Heidi had to yell over all the singing and horn tooting.

"The next stop is a visit to
Mr. Meddleboots," said the pirate.

The sea creatures cheered wildly.

"Who's Mr. Meddleboots?" asked Billy.

"Mr. Meddleboots is very clever. He
sells the sorts of things that sea creatures
love."

"What sorts of things?" asked Heidi.

"All sorts," said the pirate.
"Sou-veey-neers for the sea creatures.
And jammy bloatos for me."

"What's a jammy bloato?" asked Billy.

The pirate's eyes bulged. "Well, I'll be a mouthful of seagull's toothpaste! Don't tell me you don't know what a jammy bloato is."

"I don't know what a jammy bloato is," said Billy.

"**Butter me bathers!** Everybody knows that. Even baby sea horses.

"A jammy bloato is a pirate biscuit. They're almost as nice as porridge."

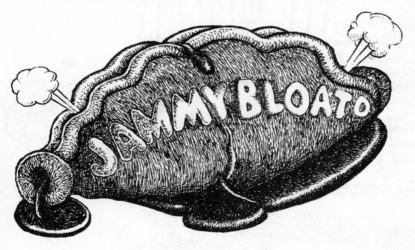

The pirate rubbed his
tummy. Then he
gave a shout.
There was a shop
up ahead. The sign
over the shop said:

MEDDLEBOOTS'
OCTOPUS GLOVES
ALL WELCOME

The pirate swerved the bus up
onto the sidewalk, skidded
over three garbage cans, and
screeched to a halt.

All of the passengers
slithered off the bus
and went through
the shop door.

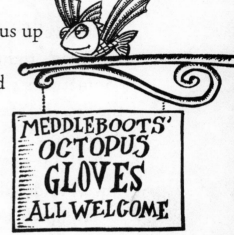

"Gloves for an octopus?" said Heidi.

"That's right," said the pirate. "Sometimes your hands get cold under the sea. Especially when you have to wave a lot."

"I didn't know that an octopus could wave," said Billy.

"Well, what do **you** do when you see a friend underwater, Mr Fishcake?"

"Umm . . ."

"You don't call out ahoy, do you? Or your mouth will fill with water. You have to wave."

"I suppose I do," said Billy.

"So does an octopus."

"I've never seen this shop before,"
said Heidi with a sniff.

"It's a floating ship, Miss Fishnose.
It's in a different spot every day."

"There's no such thing."

"There is so. Don't be such a soggy
sock! That's why Mr. Meddleboots is so
clever. He sees everything."

Just then the shop door opened again,
and all the passengers slithered and slid
back outside. They were all wearing
new clothes, and they were
looking very
pleased with
themselves.

MEDDLE BOOTS'
OCTOPUS
GLOVES
ALL WELCOME

Mr. Meddleboots came out of the shop, too. He waved to the pirate.

"Hello, Mr. Meddleboots. You're looking well. Getting over the steamroller accident, are you? You don't look as flat as the last time I saw you."

Mr. Meddleboots climbed up one step and leaned into the bus.

"Hello, Pirate," he said. "I knitted you something to say thanks for bringing all these good customers to me. I hope you like it."

He handed the pirate a long knitted tube.

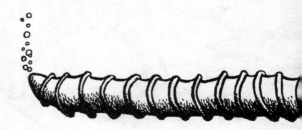

"A wooden spoon warmer! Just what I've always wanted!" The pirate whipped a spoon from his pocket and dressed it in the spoon warmer. "Thank you very much, Mr. Meddleboots."

Mr. Meddleboots looked at Billy and
Heidi.

"Hello. What have we here? Two
earwigs, I think."

"That's right," said the pirate. "Let
me introduce Miss Fishnose and Mr.
Fishcake. Watch out for Miss Fishnose,
though. We think she bites."

"I do not," said Heidi.

"Fascinating," said Mr. Meddleboots.

"Miss Fishnose will curtsy for you if you like," said the pirate.

"I will not!" exclaimed Heidi.

"Oh yes you will, Miss Fishnose," said the pirate. "Otherwise I will have to do it, and I don't know whether Mr. Meddleboots would like that."

"You'd better go along with it," whispered Billy. The thought of the pirate curtsying was quite frightening.

Heidi scowled. She walked closer to Mr. Meddleboots and curtsied. Then she shook his hand and said, "How do you do?"

Mr. Meddleboots beamed. "What strange little creatures! I must tell Mrs. Meddleboots about these talking earwigs. Speaking of which, I'm afraid I don't have your jammy bloatos, Pirate. Mrs. Meddleboots hasn't baked them yet—we didn't expect to see you so soon. We thought you'd be chasing your ship."

"My ship!" roared the pirate. "You've seen it?"

"Why yes," said Mr. Meddleboots. "I saw it just yesterday. Not very far away at all, in fact—just over the horizon there." He pointed. "Stolen again, I presume?"

The pirate growled. "That's right. But who by? Who by?

Who stole my ship, the SS *You Beauty*?"

Then Frank Fellover, Mr. Meddleboots, and the pirate all saluted.

Mr. Meddleboots shook his head sadly before he answered.

"I'm afraid your ship has been stolen by . . . monkey-crabs."

"Oh, blow me pants down!" yelled the pirate. **"Not monkey-crabs!"**

Mr. Meddleboots nodded grimly.

"The worst kind of ship stealer there is! The very worst kind!" The pirate's eyes rolled.

"But I'm sure these earwigs will help you to get it back," said Mr. Meddleboots. Then he leaned forward and whispered, "Remember to beware of the whisper word." The pirate nodded.

"And now," said Mr. Meddleboots, "I must be off. I'm knitting a raincoat for a dolphin."

The pirate pushed Mr. Meddleboots
backward off the step.

"Good-bye, Mr. Meddleboots,"
he cried as the engine roared. "See you
next time."

The bus took off with a screech.

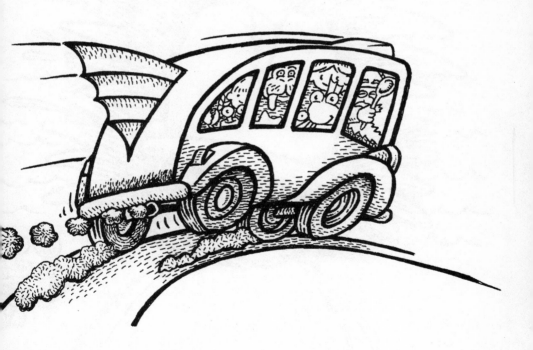

Soon, they were at the beach—headed
straight for the water. . . .

When they had reached the deepest
part of the ocean, the pirate threw open
the door.

"Attention, passengers! That is the end of our tour. Tell all your friends about it, and how wonderful I am.

"Now everybody off!"

The passengers all slithered to the door. The prawns put on their goggles, then slid below the water. The octopuses spun around in circles as they jumped out. Soon, the bus was empty.

Almost.

The pirate tapped his foot.

"You, too, Mr. Mudskipper. Get off the bus."

From behind a seat, the mudskipper smiled sheepishly at the pirate. Then he slid reluctantly up the aisle and out the door.

"You have to watch these blue-spotted mudskippers," said the pirate. "They love being on buses. They'll do anything to get a free ride."

Billy squinted out to sea.

"Um, Pirate," he said. "Look at that ship. It's going very fast."

The pirate looked.

"Oh, cake overboard! It's the SS *You Beauty*. It's mine . . . it's mine . . . bring it back . . . bring it back! Confounded monkey-crabs. And look! They have hoisted their own flag.

"That's it! That's just it! Full sails ahead! Let's go get my ship!!!"

Finally, they drew close to the
SS *You Beauty*. The monkey-crab flag was
blowing in the wind. Billy and Heidi
could see it clearly.

"Right, sailors," said the pirate.
"We will all climb quietly onto the ship.
No noise. Frank, no falling over."

Just then, they heard a little squeak. It
was the blue-spotted mudskipper. He
was sitting halfway down the bus,
pretending he was the driver.

"Rattle me collarbone! I should have
known you'd climb back on board."

The pirate turned to Billy. "See what I mean? You just can't trust these mudskippers.

"Okay, you," he said to the mudskipper. "To the back of the bus. And no hanging out the window."

"Twoink!" said Polly.

"Yes, it **is** a nice poncho he is wearing."

The pirate turned back to Billy and Heidi.

"Now, abandon bus!"

"But what about the monkey-crabs?" asked Heidi.

"Don't let them whisper in my ear!" yelled the pirate. "Don't let them whisper in Frank's ear, either.

"I had a piece of cabbage stuck in my ear once, for a whole year. I was saving it for a picnic. But it fell out. I wish it were still there, because then I wouldn't be able to hear anything that the monkey-crabs say."

"Why don't you want to hear what they say?" asked Billy.

"Feather me swordfish, Mr. Fishcake! That's a secret! Nothing for you to worry about. Now let's go!"

Billy, Heidi, Polly, Frank Fellover, and the pirate scrambled up a rope hanging over the side of the SS *You Beauty*.

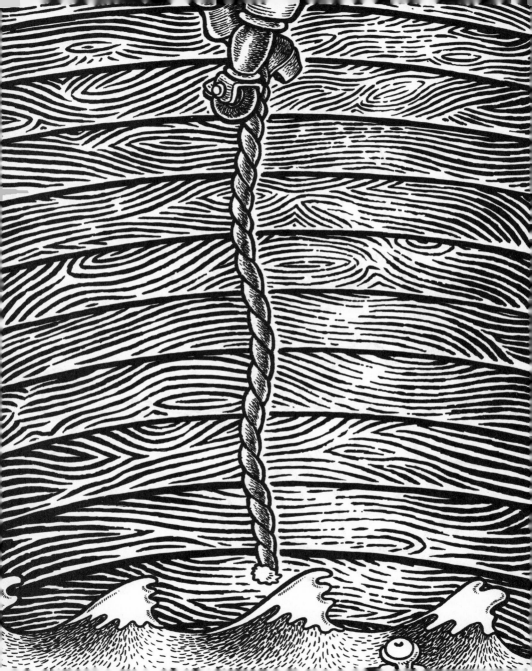

As soon as they reached the deck, monkey-crabs began to appear from every hole and dark corner of the ship.

They swung down from the masts and off the rigging, knocking over barrels and cans and anything else that was in their way.

They rollicked all over the ropes and riggings. . . .

They danced across the deck, and cartwheeled in the canvas. . . .

There were hundreds of them. The ship was a sea of monkey-crabs.

And they were all whispering something.

"Pirate panic attack! Pirate panic attack! Oh, my ears!" yelled the pirate.

One of the monkey-crabs jumped onto his shoulder and whispered in his ear.

And with that, he fell to the ground.

"What on earth is wrong with him?" said Heidi. She poked the pirate with her toe. He let out a little snore.

"What should we do?" asked Billy. A monkey-crab was hanging from his T-shirt.

Then from off in the corner there came a terrible sound. It was less than singing, but more than yelling. It reminded Billy of when he had accidentally stood on the cat next door.

"Twoink twoink twoink!
"Twoink twoink twoink?
"Twwwooink!"

It was Polly, standing by the rail with her eyes closed and her head held high. Singing.

"*What* is she doing?" asked Billy.

"It sounds horrible," said Heidi.

But all the crabs had turned toward Polly. Slowly, they began to scuttle over to her. They loved her singing!

Monkey-crabs everywhere looked at each other and nodded their heads. This was good crab singing. They moved closer, swaying in front of Polly, with their claws held up in the air.

"Twoink? Twoink? Twoink?
"Twoink. Twoink. Twoink.
"Twwoooooink!!!!"

The monkey-crabs started to chant.

"What are they saying?" Heidi yelled over all the noise.

"I'm not really sure," Billy yelled back. He leaned down to check on the pirate. "But it sounds a bit like they're all saying—*nincompoop*."

The pirate stirred, opened his eyes, blinked twice, and stretched out his arms.

"Oh," he said. "Oh yes. Porridge. Who am I? Who are you? It's not bath time, is it? No, it's save-the-ship time. Thank goodness for that. What's going on?"

He wobbled to his feet.

"They keep saying *nincompoop*," said
Heidi. And with that, the pirate fell asleep
where he stood. He began to snore.

"Oh, dear," said Billy. "You don't think
it's that word, do you? Maybe that's the
whisper word?"

"What word?" said Heidi. *"Nincompoop?"*

The pirate woke up. "I had a lovely
dream. I dreamed I was the only pirate on
the moon."

Another monkey-crab jumped onto his
shoulder. It whispered in his ear, and he
toppled over backward.

Billy looked at Heidi nervously. Heidi quickly surveyed the ship.

"We're going to have to do something, Billy," she said. "I think it's up to us."

"Right. First we'll throw the anchor overboard. Then we'll bring down the sails."

They ran to the front of the ship. The anchor was heavy, but they heaved it up, and, on the count of three, they threw it overboard.

It made a big splash, but the monkey-crabs didn't notice. They were too busy listening to Polly.

Then Billy and Heidi took the sails down. The ship stopped moving. The monkey-crabs didn't notice that, either.

The children returned to the pirate.

"We'd better say the word to wake him," said Billy.

"I suppose so," said Heidi. "You do it."

Billy leaned over to the pirate's ear and said the word. But this time, he didn't stir.

"Try again," said Heidi. "A bit louder."

Billy tried again, but nothing happened, except the snoring grew louder.

"Louder."

"Nincompoop!"

The pirate stirred.

"Once more," Heidi advised.

"NINCOMPOOP!"

The pirate's eyes opened. He tried to clear his head by shaking his arm. It worked.

He leaped up into the air. **"Bums up! Bums up!** Now the first thing we have to do is throw the anchor overboard. Then we have to take in the sails."

Heidi raised an eyebrow. "We've already done that, Pirate."

"Of course I have," said the pirate. Then he stopped and put one hand to his ear. He'd just noticed the music.

"Well, blow me cake over!" he boomed.
"My Polly must be a crab-singer. I never
knew. **What a parrot!**"

He held a megaphone up to his lips.
His voice boomed out above Polly's
singing.

"All aboard! Crab-singing,
sightseeing tour now
departing! Special deal for
monkey-crabs. I repeat.
Special deal for monkey-crabs.

"Hurry! Roll up. This bus can carry only seven hundred crabs! All aboard!

"As a special treat, this bus will be driven by a blue-speckled mudskipper. Hurry! Don't be last! All aboard!"

Polly stopped singing. For a moment all was still. Then the monkey-crabs scurried past the pirate and climbed over the side of the ship to where the bus was waiting.

And it was true! The blue-speckled mudskipper was sitting in the driver's seat, ready to go.

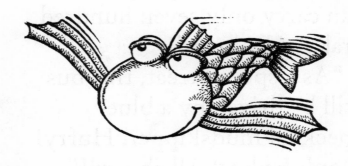

Polly and the pirate stood at the rail
and waved good-bye as the bus drove
away. They both turned and saluted.
Billy and Heidi smiled.

"And now," said the pirate, "I have a surprise for you, Mr. Fishcake. And for you, Miss Fishnose."

"A surprise!" said Billy.

"A surprise?" said Heidi.

"That's right," said the pirate. He cleared his throat, then he spoke into the megaphone.

"It is my pleasure, as captain of the SS *You Beauty*"—he saluted—"to award the Golden Cabbage Medal for Services Rendered to Pirates and Bus Drivers— a deep-sea honor never given before to somebody who wasn't a kickball champion . . ."

He raised his wooden spoon in the air gloriously.

". . . to me."

The pirate crossed his arms and nodded his head proudly.

"So three cheers for me. Hip hip . . ."

"Hooray!" yelled Frank Fellover.

"Hip hip . . ."

"Twoink!" called Polly.

"Hip hip . . ."

"Nincompoop!" yelled Heidi.

The pirate went to sleep. So did Frank Fellover.

"Now let's sail this ship home," Heidi said to Billy. "School might not be over yet. Let's sail it to school."

"Good idea," said Billy.

"Twoink," said the pig.

And do you know what? They did.